P9-CKF-851

I WANT A MONSTER!

ELISE GRAVEL

KATHERINE TEGEN BOOKS
An Imprint of HarperCollins Publishers

For Sophie and Marie,
the cutest monsters ever

Katherine Tegen Books is an imprint of HarperCollins Publishers.

I Want a Monster!

Copyright © 2016 by Elise Gravel. All rights reserved. Manufactured in China.

No part of this book may be used or reproduced in any manner whatsoever without

written permission except in the case of brief quotations embodied in critical articles

and reviews. For information address HarperCollins Children's Books, a division

of HarperCollins Publishers, 195 Broadway, New York, NY 10007.

www.harpercollinschildrens.com

ISBN 978-0-06-241533-2

The artist used Photoshop and a graphic tablet (Cintiq) to create the digital illustrations for this book.

Typography by Martha Rago

15 16 17 18 19 SCP 10 9 8 7 6 5 4 3 2 1

❖

First Edition

All my friends have pet

MONSTERS.

THIS IS
ME,

WINNIE.

Louise has an

OGG.

Simon has a

GOPTER.

Alice has a

BLOCKTOPUS.

And I want one, too. It's not fair.
I tell Papa I want a monster.

PLEASE, PLEASE, PRETTY PLEASE?

BAMBI EYES

A MONSTER?

We don't have room for a monster!

"Look, Papa, I know everything about monsters. I did my research. **I'M A MONSTER EXPERT."**

Papa takes me to the Monsterium.
This is the best day of my

LIFE!

I just love the Monsterium. I could spend my whole life in there. They have so many awesome things.

MONSTER
EGGS
→

MONSTER
FOOD!

MONSTER
PUFFS!

POTATO
JUICE

And best of all:

BABY

MONSTERS!

They have

HUNDREDS

of species:

LONG-FOOTED
PLURPS

(cute but incredibly smelly)

POOPLES

(cuddly and slimy,
eat flies)

GURKS

(very curious and
clever, might read
your diary)

MiNi-GOGS

(tiny but
very messy)

MOOGS
(strong, noisy, love sports, especially hockey)

FROOPS
(funny and very excitable, love to dance and scream)

MUSTACHIOED ZUPS
(good dressers, elegant, but smelly feet)

GIANT FOFFLES
(soft, sweet, love reading books and smelling flowers)

Papa has a crush on this little guy.
Isn't he absolutely adorable? He's a baby

OOGLY-WUMP.

According to my book, Oogly-Wumps are cuddly with red
hair, and they smell a bit like pirate feet.

"We'll name him Gus," says Papa.

Whoa! Baby monsters are something else, let me tell you.

Also, they seem to

NEVER SLEEP.

EVER.

I'm glad I have my book. It tells me everything I have to do to train and raise Gus. Here's what I learned:

**1** Monsters need lots of cuddles and hugs and kisses. That's important.

2 Otherwise, they might do silly stuff to get your attention.

POTATO POTATO POTATO POTATO POTATO POTATO POTATO POTATO PO POTATO POTATO

STOP IT, GUS!

3 Monsters eat a lot. And they eat yucky stuff!

4 They also need a bit of discipline. That's the part I'm not too good at.

Monsters grow so fast! Look at how big and healthy Gus is now. I can't believe he was a tiny baby just three weeks ago.

He doesn't do too many silly things anymore.

He might still make little mistakes from time to time.
That's normal.

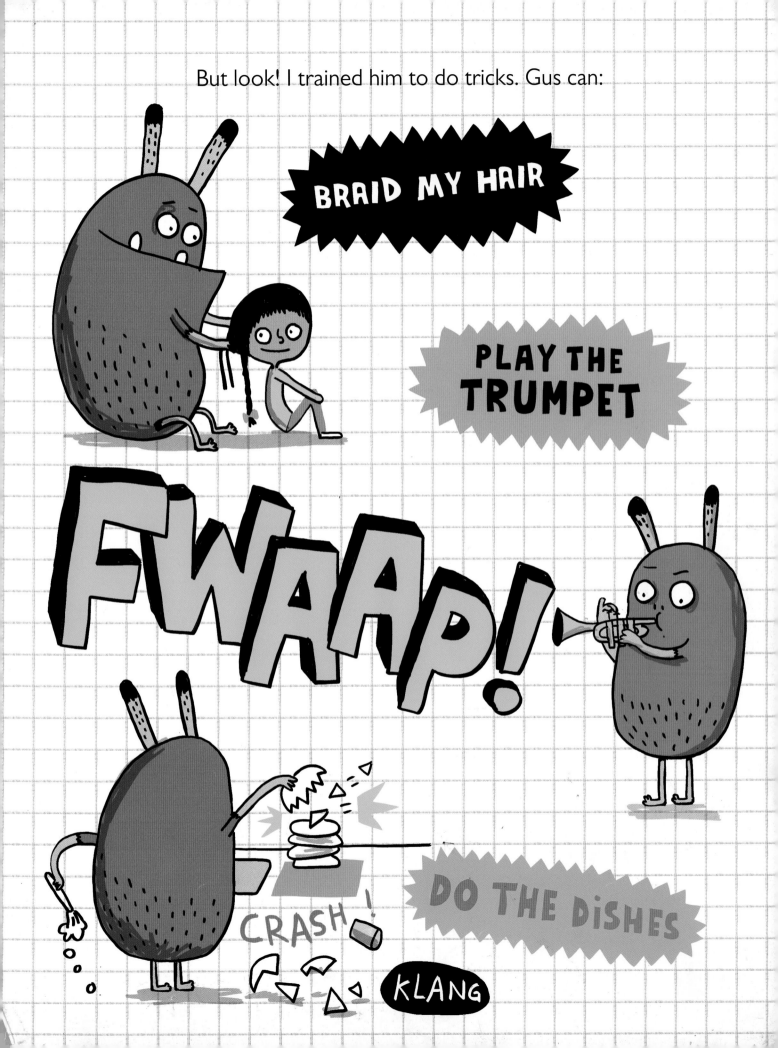

What a big, handsome, well-behaved monster! Yes, you are.

I don't like this one bit. He must be sick or something. What do they say about this in the book?

"Your monster is using bad words?"

No, that's not it.

"Your monster keeps picking his nose?"

Nope. Ah! Here it is.

"Your monster is too calm and even a little bit boring."

I found it.